UP IN THE AIR

Text copyright © 1989 by Myra Cohn Livingston
Illustrations copyright © 1989 by Leonard Everett Fisher
All rights reserved
Printed in the United States of America
First Edition

LIBRARY OF CONGRESS
Library of Congress Cataloging-in-Publication Data

Livingston, Myra Cohn.
Up in the air : poetry / by Myra Cohn Livingston ; paintings by
Leonard Everett Fisher — 1st ed.
p.   cm.

Summary: A poem describing the sights and sensations of flying in
an airplane.

ISBN 0-8234-0736-5
1. Flight—Juvenile poetry.   2. Airplanes—Juvenile poetry.
3. Children's poetry, American. [1. Flight—Poetry. 2. Airplanes—
Poetry. 3. American poetry.]   I. Fisher, Leonard Everett, ill.
II. Title.
PS3562.I945U6 1989
811′.54—dc19   88-23293   CIP   AC
ISBN 0-8234-0736-5

UP IN THE AIR

Myra Cohn Livingston

illustrated by Leonard Everett Fisher

Holiday House / New York

Good-bye to the airport! Good-bye to the ground!
My seatbelt is buckled tightly around.
The airplane is full of a roaring sound.

Faster and faster and faster we race
Over the earth and up into space,
Everyone sitting in one small place.

Off to the blue of the highest sky,
A thin curl of clouds passes us by.
Ruffled clouds chasing us, up we fly.

The airport is gone; the grasses grow small.
We leave the ground until nothing at all
Is left of the runway. Nothing at all.

Dipping and circling, climbing we go
Over the ocean. Far below
Waves wrinkle together, gray and slow.

Out of my window, the pictures change.
Far off, the peaks of a mountain range
Hold giant faces, purple and strange.

Jigsaw pieces, dumped upside down
Thrown in a jumble of country and town
Lie in a puzzle of yellow and brown.

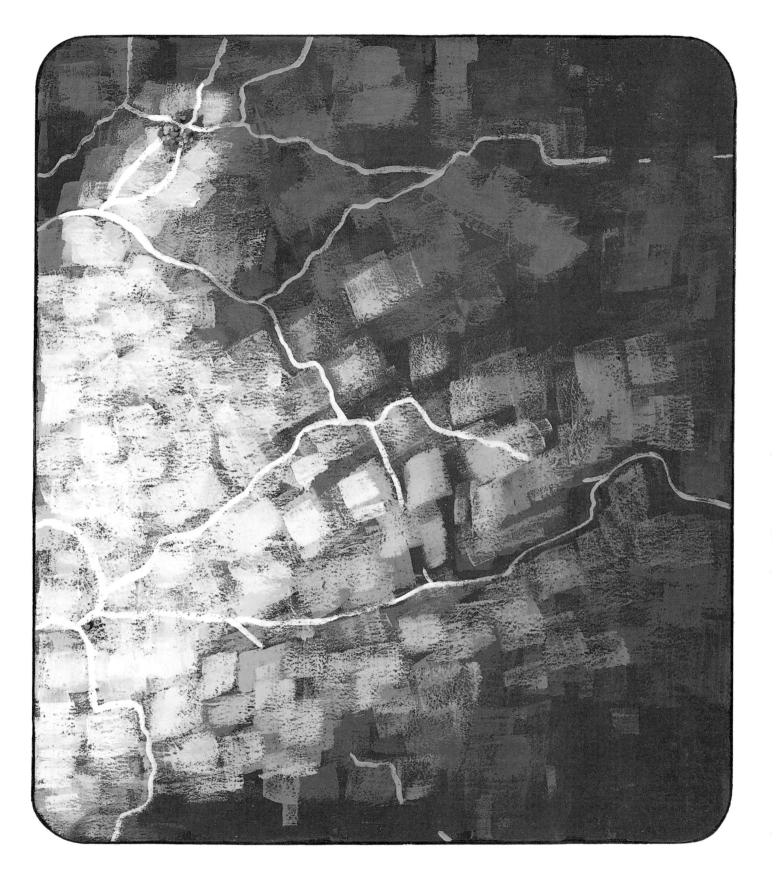

Specks of sunlight bounce in the air.
White ropes of road unwind everywhere.
A village huddles in one small square.

Lakes finger out like a giant hand.
Stepping-stones leapfrog across the land.
Shadows sunbathe on desert sand.

Hills, like sandpiles, stand beside
Umbrella forests that cover and hide
Roofs and houses and people inside.

Pink rocks blossom like roses of stone.
Gulleys turn into white, bleached bone.
Highways ride on their way alone.

Blue sky vanishes, sun slides away
Leaving a red streak in the day.
Clouds catch us, hold us, in pockets of gray.

Dropping, the earth grows big. We go
Lower and lower, and up from below
Lights of the city dance and glow.

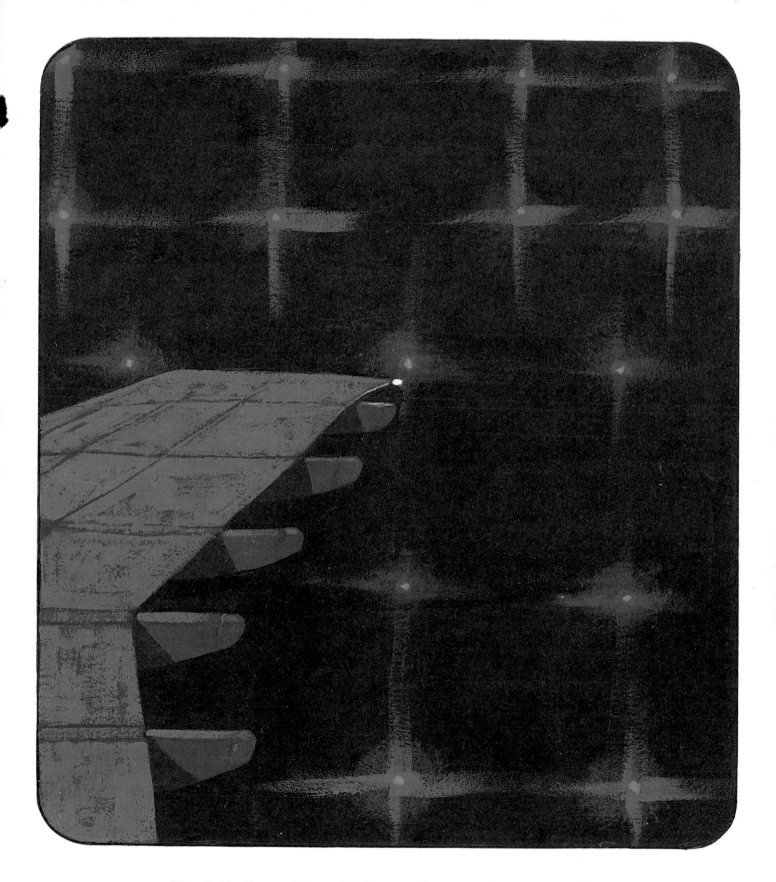

Red lights, blue lights spin on the ground,
My seatbelt is buckled tightly around.
We come from the sky in a roaring sound.

Faster and faster and faster we race.
Good-bye to sky and good-bye to space.
Hello to Earth in another place!